Le

Creati... music

Bo... gor

Illustrated by Dee Shulman
videoclips filmed by Jamie Acton-Bond

A & C Black

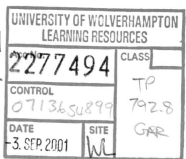

CD Audio track numbers

 Videoclip numbers

First published 2001
A & C Black (Publishers) Ltd
37 Soho Square, London W1D 3QZ

ISBN 0-7136-5489-9

Music text © Helen MacGregor
Dance text © Bobbie Gargrave
Illustrations © Dee Shulman
Cross-curricular ideas by the authors, with additional ideas by Ann Peet and Nikki Tilson
Edited and developed by Sheena Roberts
Designed by Dorothy Moir and Jocelyn Lucas
Videoclips filmed and edited by Jamie Acton-Bond
CD mastered by Jamie Acton-Bond
CD/videoclips compilation © A & C Black
Printed in Great Britain by St Edmundsbury Press Ltd, Bury St Edmunds, Suffolk

CONTENTS

Introduction   **page 4**
Using the enhanced CD   **page 5**

LET'S GO ZUDIE-O   page 6

 Zudie-o
Afro-American playground game

Dance   introducing a range of movement vocabulary; performing repeated patterns.
Music   developing a sense of rhythm through physical movement, then on simple instruments.

UPBEAT   page 10

 Country dance
18th century orchestral music

Dance   freely improvised body actions inspired by using outdoor play equipment.
Music   further development of a sense of rhythm using instruments.

MOON WALKING   page 14

 Mare tranquillitatis
20th century electronic music

Dance   free, non-rhythmical whole body movements.
Music   exploring long sounds with voices then with instruments.

THE SNOW IS DANCING   page 18

 The snow is dancing
Impressionist piano music
Dance   working with a clear contrast of weight, ie light and heavy movements.
Music   exploring contrast between high and low sounds.

CIRCLES   page 22

 Kantele
traditional Finnish zither music

Dance   making continuous flowing movement using parts of the body, and using the whole body.

Music   playing repeating patterns on tuned percussion.

IN THE GARDEN   page 26

 Playful pizzicato
20th century music for string orchestra

Dance   contrasting speed and weight.

Music   creating music with a junk instrument band.

KITCHEN FUN   page 30

 Celebrations after good harvest
traditional Chinese orchestral music

Dance   making repeated patterns of movement.

Music   working in groups to create a sound sequence.

AWAKENING   page 34

 Raga Abhogi
classical Indian music for flute and tabla

Dance   introducing and using gesture; developing representational movement to tell a story.

Music   playing freely in contrast with playing a beat; telling a story in sound.

DANCE FROM A DISTANT PLANET   page 38

 Jig
late 20th century music

Dance   moving different parts of the body in response to sound; ordering movement into a simple dance.

Music   improvising different ways of playing tuned instruments to match movements.

PARACHUTE   page 42

 Bransle de chevaux
French medieval dance music

Dance   Learning and then creating a circle dance (with or without a parachute) which is repeated at different speeds.

Music   playing a drone; playing tuned and untuned instruments at different speeds.

CIRCUS RING   page 46

 Circus music
20th century American film music

Dance   using a wide variety of movement vocabulary to create simple dance motifs to depict characters.

Music   matching sounds to movements.

JACK AND THE GIANT
                            page 50

 Contredanse
French 18th century court music

Dance – creating a narrative dance.
Music – telling a story in sound.

Dance glossary   page 54
Acknowledgements   page 55
Index of videoclips   page 56

INTRODUCTION

THE DANCE ACTIVITIES

These offer an opportunity for children to move imaginatively and expressively. The experiences will support, develop and enhance the children's access to the aesthetic, creative and physical curriculum. Through participation in the dance activities they will be presented with the opportunities to respond in movement and build their movement vocabulary. These experiences will enable them to use their movement to express ideas, feelings, moods and characters.

The music and dance experiences are mutually supportive, although exploration of the discrete areas of learning can be valuable.

The activities suggested are flexible and should be planned for delivery according to the age, stage and needs of children. All of the activities suggest initial **exploration** and improvisation work which then progresses through specific **development** tasks. It may be appropriate to engage younger children in the initial explorations only. The idea could be revisited at a later stage to increase their opportunities to learn how to develop movement.

The range of experiences found in the book draw upon ideas and stimuli from a variety of times , places and cultures in order to expose the children to greater knowledge and understanding of the world around us.

Engaging the children in these creative experiences can lead to the development of other areas of learning, and stimulate further work based on their interest.

THE MUSIC-MAKING ACTIVITIES

These offer children a variety of opportunities to explore sounds made with the voice, bodies, untuned and tuned percussion and junk instruments. The activities are closely related to the dance ideas but can be explored separately if you wish. They are intended to be flexible – it is not necessary to complete all the activities suggested, and you and the children will have ideas of other ways to develop the music-making, dance and listening. The amount of time you spend on each activity and frequency of repetitions will depend on each group of children. You will need to judge the readiness of your own particular group of children for each of the exploratory and development activities. The **explorations** may be sufficiently demanding for younger children, but can be revisited at a later date when the children are ready to work more independently and move onto the **developments**.

When you have begun to explore the music-making activities of a particular piece, you may like to leave photocopies of the illustrations in a music corner, along with the recording and a collection of appropriate instruments or sound sources. In this way the children will be able to play with the ideas and devise improvisations, games and compositions for themselves.

USING THE MUSIC RECORDINGS ON THEIR OWN

The twelve pieces of music have been carefully chosen to introduce young children to a wide variety of musical styles from different places and times which will broaden their experience of listening to music. The pieces can be used independently of the suggested activities to give children opportunities to respond spontaneously to what they hear through movement, words or paint. Play a chosen piece (without revealing the title or theme of the linked activities) to explore what the children notice and how they react. Some children will want to describe their feelings, ideas, likes and dislikes through language, while others will find it easier to express their reactions through other media. Remember responses will be unique to each child – some may describe pictures they have imagined as they listen, others may recognise an instrument they have heard before, others will not be able to articulate their feelings in words, but may want to move as they listen.

The suggested dance and musical activities lead the children towards more focussed listening and a greater understanding of the music: patterns, structures and elements (eg loud and quiet sounds, fast and slow sounds) and the wide range of sounds made by different instruments.

Give the children plenty of opportunities to listen independently to pieces you have begun to explore with them. Place a CD or cassette player and recordings of the music in a music corner.

THE VIDEOCLIPS

The videoclips are for both you and for the children to view. The clips of the Apollo moon landings, the Chinese dragon dancing in the streets of Soho, or Shaila Thiru's demonstrations of Asian dance movements are visually intriguing in their own right.

Many of the clips show unrehearsed explorations of the activities, performed by teachers and children. They are not final performances, but exemplifications of how you might begin your work together. While these may be of particular use to you, you may also like to show them to the children to stimulate discussion and develop their ideas.

USING THE ENHANCED CD

Your CD is both a conventional audio CD and a CD ROM.

USING A CD PLAYER TO PLAY THE AUDIO TRACKS

The CD will play on any conventional CD player – use it just as you would any other music CD.

Track numbers

Some of the pieces of music have more than one section. To help you find the sections, we have given them separate track numbers. For example, the three sections of Circus Music are numbered 16, 17 and 18. To go to the middle section of the music, simply select track 17.

To hear the complete piece of music unbroken, select track 16 and let the music continue playing through to the end of track 18 (there are no gaps between these three tracks).

USING A COMPUTER TO PLAY THE AUDIO TRACKS AND THE VIDEOCLIPS

Audio tracks

The audio tracks may be played on a computer. Insert the CD into your CD drive, and open the tracks through your CD player.

Videoclips

Videoclips are for viewing on a computer. They are in a format called MPEG-1, a widely used movie format supported on most computer desktops including both PC and Mac.

Most computers have an installed movie player, eg Windows Media Player on a PC; QuickTime on a Mac. However the procedure for opening a videoclip may vary from one computer to another. Follow the opening procedure for your particular computer.

If your computer does not have a ready-installed movie player, you may download one of the many free players available on the Internet. Go to download.com to find one.

The index at the back of the book describes the content of each videoclip.

LET'S GO ZUDIE-O

Zudie-o *is an Afro-American playground game. Individual children choose a locomotive movement – walking, skipping, striding – which they take turns to perform, travelling up and down between two facing lines of children. The children in the lines then copy the locomotive movement on the spot.*

Dance

The children experience and perform a range of locomotive movements, developing a physical sense of rhythm.

Music

They match instrumental sounds to quality of movement, eg playing heavy sounds on tambour to match a heavy stamping movement. Later they play the sounds as the dance is performed.

Resources

– Small hand-held percussion instruments such as shakers and drums.

Preparation

Sing the song together, using CD Track 1 to learn the melody and words.

Watch the videoclip alone or with the children to familiarise yourselves with the structure of the game.

walk

jump

creep

jog

skip

hop

gallop

march

turn

trot

* * * * * * *

Let's go zudie-o, zudie-o, zudie-o,
Let's go zudie-o all night long.

Stand in two facing lines and clap the beat *****, while Sally chooses and performs an action - she walks up and down between the lines.

We're walking through the valley,
  the valley, the valley
We're walking through the valley,
  all night long.

Sally continues to walk up and down, while the others copy her movement on the spot.

Step back, Sally, Sally, Sally,
Step back, Sally all night long.

Sally goes back to her place in line.

And here comes another one,
  another one another one,
And here comes another one,
  all night long.

The next child (Missak) steps out.

Let's go zudie-o, zudie-o, zudie-o ...

Missak chooses to jump along.

We're jumping through the valley ...

The children copy Missak's movements on the spot.

Step back, Missak, Missak, Missak ...

Missak steps back into line and the game continues.

DANCE EXPLORATION

- Explore (without the song) a range of locomotive movements which can be performed on the spot and travelling, eg

  - walking
  - marching
  - skipping
  - jumping
  - hopping
  - turning
  - creeping

- Choose a locomotive movement and sing one of the action verses together, eg

  We're **walking** through the valley,
     the valley, the valley,
  We're **walking** through the valley,
     all night long.

  Everyone walks rhythmically, first on the spot, then travelling around the space.

- Change to a different movement, eg **marching**. Perform this with strong, firm movements.

- Change again, continuing to move rhythmically, and in a way which reflects the quality of the word, eg **creeping** – move quietly and lightly.

1 LET'S GO ZUDIE-O

Listen to the song and travel during the action verses, using the appropriate locomotive movements and qualities. Sing the other sections of the song standing on the spot, clapping the beat.

MUSIC EXPLORATION

The children sit, each with a small untuned percussion instrument placed in front of them (a maraca for each child if possible).

- Direct one child, Sally, to perform one of the locomotive movements (without the song).

- While Sally moves, you lead the other children in making a sound which matches the movement, eg

Sally walks	you tap the maraca on alternate knees – the children copy
Ravi marches	you tap the maraca firmly on the palm of your hand – the children copy
Ben skips	'skip' the maraca in the air
Olu jumps	'jump' the maraca high and bring down on the palm
Shaila hops	small, short, heavy taps on the thigh
Bunma turns	swirl in circles
Sam creeps	little fingertip taps on the surface of the maraca

- Everyone stands, each holding their maracas ready to play. Sing the action verses of the song, using the instrumental sounds you have explored for each action.

1 LET'S GO ZUDIE-O

Listen to the song and join in using the appropriate sounds on the instruments during the action verses. Sing the other sections of the song, keeping the instruments still.

DANCE DEVELOPMENT

● Teach the whole song and the whole game structure. The aim is to be confident in singing the song and performing the actions unaccompanied.

● When the children can confidently perform the singing game with the locomotive movements explored so far, they can begin creating new movements, eg wiggling through the valley, sliding, flapping, flying, and so on.

MUSIC DEVELOPMENT

● Ask individual children to demonstrate their new movements while the other children explore sounds on their instruments to match.

PERFORMANCE

Perform the whole singing game with the instruments. Individual children choose their own movements and their own sounds for the others to copy during the action verses. Everyone takes their instrument and stands in line. Sally walks between the lines, making walking sounds on her maraca. Everyone copies.

CROSS-CURRICULAR LINKS

Language – make a picture of movement words – hopping, skipping, jumping, walking.

Science – look at the way animals move.

PSE – talk about taking turns.

Maths – find ways to illustrate the structure of the game, using coloured cubes or shapes, eg

Art – draw patterns using straight lines.

ICT – record the group singing the song to replay on the classroom cassette player. Talk about ways of improving the singing.

UPBEAT

Country dance *comes from The Water Music by Handel. It has a strong playful skipping rhythm. There are three sections, the middle of which is characterised by light, high sounds. The first and third sections are heavier and lower-sounding.*

Dance

The children use outdoor play equipment to explore the contrasting ways in which hoops, ropes and balls move. Then they themselves interpret the spinning hoops, swinging ropes and bouncing balls in movement.

Music

The children develop control in playing strong walking and skipping rhythms first with body percussion and then on instruments.

Resources

- Hoops and quoits, skipping ropes of different lengths, balls of different sizes and materials (rubber, sponge, airflow, plastic, tennis, football, etc).
- Enlarged copies of the stride and skip cards, page 13.
- A selection of tambours, small drums, and a cow bell.

Preparation

Let the children use the equipment in free play. Afterwards, collect vocabulary which describes the way in which the objects move. Videoclip 2 shows a range of movements, eg

hoop	forwards, backwards, turn and spin, roll around, over and under;
rope	jump, swing, wriggle;
ball	up, down, bounce, roll.

DANCE EXPLORATION

2-4 COUNTRY DANCE - HOOPS

In a large open space, the children use the movements they identified whilst playing with equipment previously:

2 As the music begins, call 'walk'. All walk to the beat of the music.

3 Call 'Hoops'. Everyone interprets a hoop and improvises freely. (You may like to call out some action words as the music plays, eg spin, roll, turn, fall.)

4 Call 'Walk' again. Everyone walks again.

● Ask some children to demonstrate their walking movements and talk about the quality of movement which matches the music – stepping strongly, swinging arms – ie striding.

2-4 COUNTRY DANCE - ROPES

Extend the walking movements by striding this time and by changing direction as the music plays.

2 Call 'Stride'. All stride strongly and purposefully, changing direction.

3 Call 'Ropes'. (Swing, sway, jump, twist.)

4 Call 'Stride'. All stride.

● Some children may be ready to explore skipping instead of striding in the first and last sections. Give the children the choice of doing either.

2-4 COUNTRY DANCE - BALLS

2 'Stride' or 'Skip'.

3 'Balls'. (Roll, turn, bounce, spin, drop.)

4 'Stride' or 'Skip'.

MUSIC EXPLORATION

The children explore playing a striding and a skipping rhythm using body percussion.

● Introduce these two sounds to the children, asking them to copy you as you clap and say 'STRIDE', then 'and SKIP':

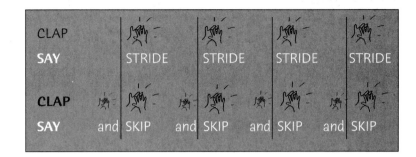

CLAP				
SAY	STRIDE	STRIDE	STRIDE	STRIDE
CLAP				
SAY	and SKIP	and SKIP	and SKIP	and SKIP

Skip switch 1 - clapping game

● You call 'STRIDE' and everyone claps. Keep clapping the steady striding beat until you call 'and SKIP' – everyone changes. (Both rhythms maintain the same pulse – the strong clap of 'SKIP' coinciding with 'STRIDE')

● Divide into two groups – striders and skippers. Call 'STRIDE' and everyone in the striding group claps the striding rhythm. Call 'and SKIP' – the striding group stops and the skipping group begins, taking up the pulse without a pause.

● Swap over so that all have practice in striding and skipping.

Skip switch 2 - percussion game

You need two sets of contrasting percussion instruments, eg drums for the striding group and tambourines for the skippers. (Hold the tambourine horizontally and tap lightly near the rim with the fingers of the writing hand.) You may reinforce the rhythms yourself by playing a cowbell or other clear-sounding instrument.

● Call (and play the rhythm on the cowbell) 'STRIDE'. The striders tap their striding rhythm on the drums. Keep going until you call and play 'and SKIP' – striders stop, skippers begin.

● Keep switching from one group to the other.

● Swap the instruments over so that all practise playing the drums and the tambourines.

DANCE DEVELOPMENT

2-4 COUNTRY DANCE

Refine the movements, encouraging the children to make a clear contrast between strong striding (or rhythmic skipping), and the light quality of the hoops, ropes and balls. Make the rolling, bouncing, spinning very light and large, using all the available space.

MUSIC DEVELOPMENT

- Play Skip Switch again, but this time encourage the children – those who are able – to use alternate hands in both the body percussion and on the instruments.

- You lead the game, choosing different parts of the body for the children to copy, but always tapping alternate hands (L/R):

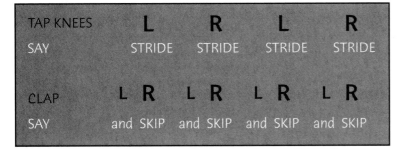

TAP KNEES	L	R	L	R
SAY	STRIDE	STRIDE	STRIDE	STRIDE
CLAP	L R	L R	L R	L R
SAY	and SKIP	and SKIP	and SKIP	and SKIP

- Make enlarged copies of the stride and skip cards, above right.

- Divide into two groups – drums and tambourines (striders and skippers). To start the groups, show the stride card first then swap to the skipping card. Alternate the cards. Each group starts and stops in response. At intervals hide both cards and all players fall silent.

Performance suggestion

STRIDE

and SKIP

PERFORMANCE

- Divide into three groups – dancers, drummers (striders) and tambourines (skippers).

- Conduct the instrument groups with the cards. When a movement card is shown, the dancers stride or skip as appropriate around the whole space, while the drums or the tambourines play.

- When you hide the cards and call 'HOOPS', 'ROPES' or 'BALLS', the instruments stop playing and the dancers change to the play movements. The chart below indicates one possible sequence. (You may prefer to dance to the recording, in which case, play tracks 2-4 three times.)

CROSS-CURRICULAR LINKS

Language – use the structure of **Country Dance** to create a group poem, eg

We walk to nursery every day,
We roll our hoops and spin them,
We walk to nursery every day.

We walk to nursery every day,
We swing the ropes and turn them,
We walk to nursery every day.

We walk to nursery every day …

Art – explore mark making through rolling hoops, ropes and balls into paint and across large sheets of paper.

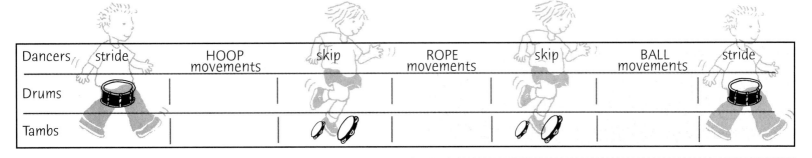

Dancers	stride	HOOP movements	skip	ROPE movements	skip	BALL movements	stride
Drums							
Tambs							

MOON WALKING

Mare Tranquillitatis _by Vangelis, is a picture in sound of the first moon landing. The composer uses electronic sounds and real recordings of astronauts talking to create a feeling of weightlessness and outer space._

Dance and music

Taking giant weightless steps as if exploring the surface of the moon, the children discover how to move smoothly, slowly and lightly. They create their own moon music, exploring ways to play overlapping layers of long smooth sounds.

Resources

- A ball, a balloon and five pots of bubble mixture.
- Instruments which can make continuous sounds (see p16).

Preparation

Watch the astronauts together. Buzz Aldrin described moon walking like this – 'I took off jogging to test my manoeuvrability. The exercise gave me an odd sensation and looked even more odd when I later saw the films of it. With bulky suits on, we seemed to be moving in slow motion. I noticed immediately that my inertia seemed much greater. Earth-bound, I would have stopped my run in just one step, but I had to use three of four steps to sort of wind down. My Earth weight, with the big backpack and heavy suit, was 360 pounds. On the Moon I weighed only 60 pounds.'

Play Moon ball

The children stand in a circle. Pass a ball to the first child, who passes it on round the circle. Draw the children's attention to the weight of the ball. Now tell them that they are astronauts playing catch on the moon. Blow up a balloon and compare its lightness with that of the ball. Throw the balloon in slow motion with a gentle swing to the first child, who slowly and gently taps it back. Continue until everyone has tapped the balloon.

DANCE EXPLORATION

● Explore a variety of actions on the spot. Contrast performing them quickly with performing them slowly as if on the moon, eg

- clap quickly; clap slowly (stretch both hands out, bringing them together in a large slow arc, touching lightly with no sound)
- wave quickly; wave slowly (both arms, fingers stretched, large slow overhead arc)
- cheer energetically and noisily; cheer soundlessly (both arms slowly raised and punching the air).
- try other movements, eg picking up a moon rock

● Explore whole body actions on the spot. Begin crouched down low, balanced on toes and hands, slowly and lightly rise up towards a tall stretch. Reverse the action and sink slowly down.

● Explore slow, large, smooth whole body actions which travel

- walking with giant weightless strides in and out of spaces, forward and backwards.
- turning

---

5 MARE TRANQUILLITATIS

As the music plays, the children move weightlessly, freely using any of the actions explored.

MUSIC EXPLORATION

Bubbles

You need a pot of bubble mixture.

● Blow some bubbles and talk about how they float and smoothly fall to the ground or pop in the air.

● Ask the children each to pick a gentle sound they can make with their voices which can last for a long time, eg

- ooooooooooooooo
- ahhhhhhhhhhhhh
- sssssssssssssssssssss
- weeeeeeeeeeeeeeee
- hummmmmmmmmm
- fooooooooooooooo
- shhhhhhhhhhhhhh

● Now ask the children to make their chosen sound as you blow a series of bubbles. When all the bubbles have popped, the children stop.

Older children may be encouraged to pick an individual bubble and follow its course with the vocal sound they have chosen.

● Transfer to instruments. Find ways of making long sounds, eg

- tambourine or drum: trace a circle round the skin with a finger
- keyboard: press one key continuously, or move without breaks to others
- blow through a straw into a plastic bottle with a little water in it
- cymbal: tap quickly and repeatedly with a soft beater
- rainstick: tip slowly
- radio: tune on and off station for voices and static
- ocean drum: swirl (or swirl a little rice or some marbles around the inside of a tambour, held skin down.)

MUSIC DEVELOPMENT

Moon bubbles

Now the object is to make a piece of recorded moon music. You will need four or five tubs of bubble mixture, and a cassette recorder.

- Divide into four or five groups each with a set of instruments (use vocal sounds if not enough instruments). Each group has a tub of bubble mixture and appoints a bubble conductor who stands in the centre holding the tub (with younger children you may wish to take this role yourself).

- When you point to a group, the bubble conductor blows a stream of bubbles. The others gently start their long sounds and keep playing until all the bubbles have disappeared.

- Before the first group finishes playing, point to the second group, and continue until all the groups have overlapped.

- Repeat the activity, changing the order of the groups. Record each complete performance.

DANCE DEVELOPMENT

Moon bubbles

You need the recording you made earlier and the cassette machine.

- Listen to and choose one of the recorded performances.

- Play the recording, while everyone moves with the moon walker actions they have already explored.

- Work on the actions to create short individual sequences of slow light movement, eg

    – rising, turning, cheering, moving about, collecting a rock, sinking down.

PERFORMANCE

Create a final performance by making a moon-walker tableau. Half the children create the rocks and craters of the moon landscape, using different body shapes: round, wide, twisted, spiky, smooth. The other half explore this moon landscape, using their moon-walking sequences.

Perform the dance either to track 5 or to the children's own recording.

CROSS-CURRICULAR LINKS

Language – read 'Whatever next!' by Jill Murphy and retell the narrative in correct sequence using props in the role play area or small world toys and DT models.

Maths – investigate circles and spheres.

Art – explore different textures through bubble painting.

DT – model a moon landscape using clay. Build rockets and space buggies using a range of construction equipment.

ICT – visit the NASA kids website (www.nasa.gov/kids) or the Apollo 11 pages at the website of the US National Air and Space Museum (www.nasm.edu/apollo/).

THE SNOW IS DANCING

The Snow is dancing *is a piece of Impressionist piano music by the French composer, Debussy. It evokes a wintry scene of falling snowflakes. Rapid light streams of notes – each an individual snowflake – create a three-dimensional effect. The snowflakes continuously flutter, swirl, rise, sink and drift. Towards the middle of the piece, the snow becomes more dense and heavy and the music is louder and stronger, but the lightness of the opening soon resumes.*

Dance

Each child explores the quality of lightness, responding freely to the music, whilst travelling and turning in their own personal space and in the larger general space. They respond to the heavier sounds in the middle section of the music and feel the contrast with the extreme lightness of the beginning and end.

Music

Everyone explores ways of playing lightly and quickly on a variety of untuned percussion instruments. Individual children, using chime bars, add simple rising and falling patterns of notes. The patterns mimic those in the music, describing flurries of snowflakes.

Resources

A selection of small untuned instruments, eg bells, finger cymbals, tambourines.
A set of chime bars – notes EFGA and beaters.
A single chime bar – note B♭ and beater.

Preparation

Watch the snow animation. Talk about snow. What does it feel like, look like? Collect snow words, using the illustration as a stimulus.

DANCE EXPLORATION

6 THE SNOW IS DANCING (OPENING)

Tell the children the name of the music then play it, asking them to imagine the movement of snowflakes. On repeated listenings, encourage the children to:

● Travel around lightly on tiptoe, in and out of each other.

● Add turning actions to the travelling.

● Tiptoe in personal space.

● Stretch the arms high above heads, looking at the hands then move them gently down towards the floor.

● Repeat the action of hands moving from high to low, adding twisting and turning movements.

MUSIC EXPLORATION

Snowflakes falling

● Give each child one of the suggested untuned percussion instruments. Listen as individual children show ways of playing their instrument to make light, quiet, fast-falling 'snowflakes'. Experiment with fingertips on tambourines, gentle shakes on bells, quiet taps on Indian bells.

● Sit in a circle. Each child, one by one, plays the sound they have found.

● Divide the circle into small groups. Each group takes a turn to play freely together, remembering to make each individual snowflake sound very quiet and gentle.

● Place the set of chime bars (E F G A) in the centre of the circle and invite a child from each group to play repeating patterns while the group continues to make snowflake sounds, eg

(low to high pitch)

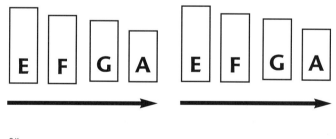

or

(high to low pitch)

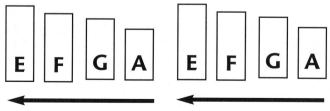

DANCE DEVELOPMENT

6 THE SNOW IS DANCING (COMPLETE)

OPENING – Snowflakes falling
As the opening music plays, perform the travelling and turning actions using the whole space. The movements should be light and continuous to reflect the quality of the music.

At 1'04" and at 1'26", a high repeated note is heard. Here the children may stop travelling but keep performing their high to low hand movements .

MIDDLE – Deep snow
At 1'18" and 1'35", the music becomes louder. Here the children find a travelling movement which is heavier and stronger, eg trudging, pushing, leaning.

ENDING – Snowflakes falling
AT 1'50" the music returns to the style of the opening, and the children resume their light, travelling movements.

MUSIC DEVELOPMENT

Deep snow footsteps – game

Give one child a single B♭ chime bar. This child signals all the others to change from playing their light, snowflake sounds to playing heavier, deep snow, footstep sounds.

Divide into groups as before. Each group chooses one child to play the set of chime bars (EFGA). The groups take turns to play.

1. One group starts playing the gentle snowflake sounds and chime bar patterns they have made.

2. At any point, the child with the B♭ chime bar may signal the change to deep snow.

3. At the signal, the group plays heavier sounds and the group's chime bar player uses both beaters to play a succession of pairs of chime bar notes.

4. The signal is heard again.

5. The light snowflake sounds resume.

PERFORMANCE

All dance to the recording, or some dance while the others provide the music you have devised together.

CROSS-CURRICULAR LINKS

Literacy – collect words associated with winter weather.
Read poems about snow and winter weather.

Geography – learn about seasons and climate.

Science – investigate freezing and melting.

Art – make a snowflakes frieze.
Look at Impressionist paintings.
Design creative snowflake patterns

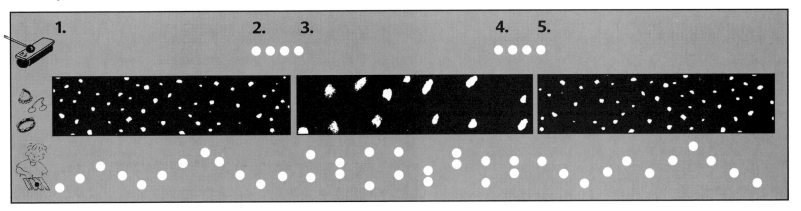

Circles

Kantele *is a piece of traditional Finnish music played on a stringed instrument called a kantele. The five strings are plucked.*

Dance

The children use the flow and quality of the music to explore continuous circular movement in the air, on the floor, and with the whole body.

Music

The children make continuous repeating patterns of notes on tuned percussion.

Resources

- Chime bars, xylophones, glockenspiels and beaters. Notes F G A B C D E.

Preparation

Talk about the pictures opposite:
- what do they do?
- how do they move?
- where do you see them?

As you talk, demonstrate the movements of each object with your hands. Draw circles in the air to show the windmill turning, spiral a fingertip to show a sycamore seed twirling to the ground.

Find and identify other objects which move in a circular way.

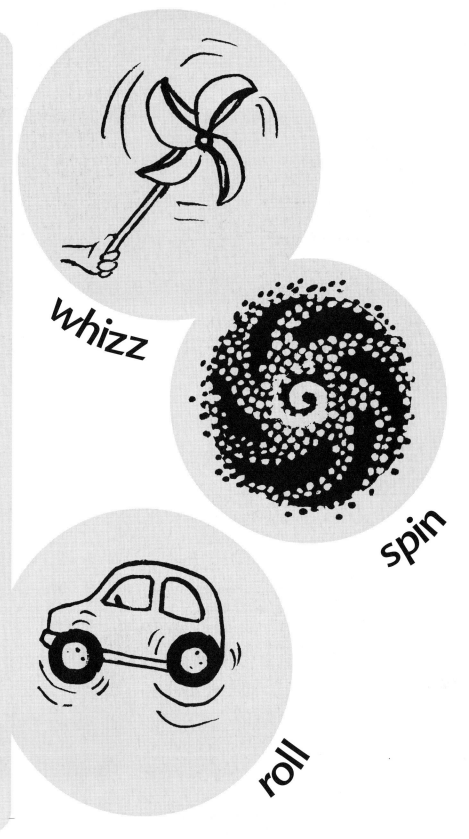

whizz

spin

roll

turn

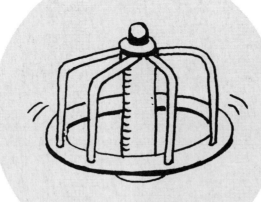

circle

rotate

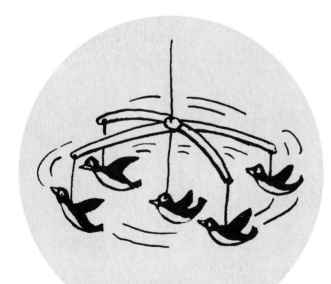

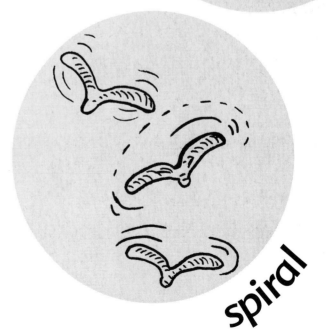

revolve

spiral

DANCE EXPLORATION

7 KANTELE

● While listening to the music, the children draw a circle in front of their bodies using the fingertips to lead the movement. Make the movement larger by bending and stretching so that the circle goes from high to low and back again.

● Try making this large circular air pattern in different places, eg above the head, to the side of the body, going around the body. Sometimes these patterns may be near to the body and sometimes, by extending the arm, further away.

● Make these air patterns using different parts of the body to lead the movement, eg elbow, nose, toes, knee. These circles may be very small or very big.

● Ask the children to imagine having paint on the soles of their feet. Can they walk a circle on the floor which finishes where it began? Travel and make floor circles in different parts of the room, eg

● Find different ways to make the whole body turn round, eg

- standing and pivoting on the spot
- jumping and turning
- rolling from knees and hands to bottom
- lying and rolling

● Find ways to travel whilst using turning actions.

MUSIC EXPLORATION

You will need tuned percussion. Arrange the tuned percussion in sets of three notes, five notes and seven notes, eg

● Arrange the set of three notes in a circle in any order you like, eg

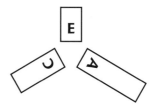

Ask the children to listen while you play the set of notes one after the other. Keep steadily repeating them over and over again:

E A C E A C E A C E ...

Encourage the children to recognise the repetition of the three notes in the pattern as they watch you play.

Now ask the children to respond to your playing by making small circles near to their bodies using different parts to lead the movement.

● Order the set of five notes into a pattern, eg

Ask the children to respond by making larger circles further away from their bodies using different parts to lead the movement.

● Order the group of seven notes to make a pattern and ask the children to respond by making circles which travel around the space, using different levels, speeds and direction.

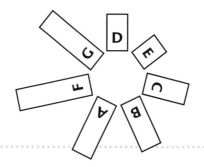

MUSIC DEVELOPMENT

You will need a table or space where the three sets of tuned percussion may be played by the children individually.

● Encourage individual children to order the notes to create their own patterns of three, five or seven notes, and to practise playing them repeatedly and steadily.

MUSIC AND DANCE DEVELOPMENT

Place the three sets of tuned percussion in the centre of the group and choose a child to play. This child orders the notes of one of the sets, then plays them one after the other, steadily and repeatedly. The others recognise the short, medium or long pattern, and respond with the appropriate movement:

- three notes: small circles near to the body
- five notes: larger circles further away
- seven notes: circular floor patterns using turning actions

Let another child take a turn to choose and play a set of notes. The other children recognise it and respond again with the appropriate movement.

PERFORMANCE

You will need a large space. Place the three sets of tuned percussion well apart from each other. Choose a child to order and play repeating patterns on each set.

The other children position themselves near a note-set of their choice. The musicians start playing. The dancers respond with the appropriate movements. They choose when to move on to another set of notes, travelling to it using circular floor patterns.

CROSS-CURRICULAR LINKS

Language – tell the story of the roll-away pancake.

Design and technology – investigate the movement of wheels.

Art – use circles to create a collage.

PSE – circle time (the importance of the circle).

Science – study life cycles

Maths – shape recognition (two-dimensional) – find examples of circles in the environment.

IN THE GARDEN

Playful pizzicato *from Simple Symphony for Strings by Benjamin Britten begins with a light and lively, busy melody, followed by a slower, heavier melody with a strong working beat. In this activity, the music sets the scene for a garden, busy with insect life, suddenly interrupted by the appearance of the gardener.*

Dance

The children work with movements of contrasting speed and weight.

Music

The children create a piece of minibeast music using junk instruments.

Resources

– The materials for the instruments are illustrated opposite. Use your own ideas for minibeast instruments as well.

Preparation

Visit a garden or watch a video to observe minibeasts: bees, butterflies, beetles, ants, grasshoppers. Notice their movements and any sounds they make. Make a list of useful movement words.

Grasshopper guiros

Rub tubes of sandpaper together.

Beetle bongos

crick crack

Tap together two smooth round pebbles.

jump flap fly flutter flit

The minibeast band

Cricket fiddle

Stretch elastic bands round a strong box.

Twang Twang Twang

Ant maraca

Pour lentils into an empty film canister.

checka check checka check

Butterfly flapper

Tie tissue paper round a chopstick then slit.

frrr frrr frrr frrr

Bee kazoo

Hum through thin paper folded over a new comb.

Bzzzzz

hover   glide   stretch   rub   scuttle   curl   crawl   hop

DANCE EXPLORATION

The insects

- The children individually choose one of the minibeast movement words and travel freely around the room weaving in and out of others, keeping all movements light and quick.

- Change from travelling to moving on the spot using just hands and arms, eg show a beetle scuttling then digging; a butterfly fluttering then landing and moving antennae or wings; a dragonfly flitting then hovering; an ant scurrying then eating.

> **⑧ PLAYFUL PIZZICATO (FIRST SECTION)**
>
> **As the music plays, the children make the movements they have explored.**
>
> **Repeat the pattern of travelling and moving on the spot, remembering to reflect the quality of the music – light, fine, quick.**

The gardeners

- The children find ways of travelling around the room using slow, heavy actions to represent the gardeners, eg stomping in boots, wheeling a barrow, carrying heavy buckets.

- Now they explore making working actions within the limit of their personal space, eg digging, raking side to side or in and out, hoeing, chopping a hedge, sawing logs, sowing seeds.

- Next they make a sequence of travelling followed by working on the spot.

> **⑨ PLAYFUL PIZZICATO (SECOND SECTION)**
>
> **The children create the gardener's movements while the music plays.**

MUSIC EXPLORATION

The minibeast band

- Make the instruments suggested on pp24-25. Add your own and the children's ideas.

- Explore the sounds of each instrument – how quietly/quickly can it be played.

- Let the children form small minibeast bands together, eg one ant, one beetle, one bee, one butterfly. Encourage them to

  - play in turn
  - combine two sounds
  - play all together

(The diagram opposite shows an example of one of these explorations.)

DANCE DEVELOPMENT

In the garden

> **8-10 PLAYFUL PIZZICATO (COMPLETE)**
>
> **As the complete piece of music plays, create your garden scene.**
>
> **⑧ Busy insects travelling and stopping. As the music pauses at the end of this section, the insects freeze into stillness.**
>
> **⑨ One or more gardeners enter and work. As the music pauses again, the gardeners flop to the ground to munch their sandwiches.**
>
> **⑩ The insects busily resume their activities, while the gardeners quietly watch. Towards the very end, the gardeners can't help themselves but jump up and join in.**

MUSIC DEVELOPMENT

The minibeast band and the gardeners

● Ask the children each to paint a picture of the garden showing the minibeasts and the gardener.

● In small groups they then create music for one of the pictures, telling the story of **In the garden**. They will need to find instruments for the gardeners. Use classroom instruments or junk instruments which contrast clearly in size and volume with the minibeast band.

● Ask different groups to perform their music for the others.

CROSS-CURRICULAR LINKS

Language – read Eric Carle's stories about minibeasts, eg 'The Very Hungry Caterpillar', 'The Bad-Tempered Ladybird', 'The Very Busy Spider'. Make class books, transposing ideas from the stories you have read.

Language and PSE – ask the children to write letters to the Bad-Tempered Ladybird, suggesting ways to be polite and friendly.

Maths – play the beetle game using dice and paper.
Count body parts, eg legs on spiders.
Make playdough worms of different lengths and use standard units to measure them. Introduce vocabulary such as longer than/shorter than.
Make a ladybird domino game. Can the children match the spots?
Using data from the minibeast hunt (see below), make a tally chart or graph of what you have found.

ICT – visit the Eric Carle website (www.eric-carle.com).
Use a painting programme such as RM Colour Magic to make minibeast pictures.

Art – make 3D minibeasts using clay or salt dough.

Science – go on a minibeast hunt around the grounds of the school, carefully recording what was found and where.
Make close observations of minibeasts, eg stick insects, snails; record observations in drawings and label body parts.
Learn new vocabulary associated with the different species.

Geography – make a map of the minibeast hunt.
Look at different habitats.

KITCHEN FUN

Celebrations after good harvest *is a piece of exuberant Chinese music. It is played on the traditional string, wind and percussion instruments of a Chinese village orchestra.*

Dance

The children compose an action-packed stir fry dance for a celebration feast. They use hand actions then whole body actions, creating simple repeatable patterns. Later, there is the opportunity to develop a dragon dance.

Music

Cooking actions are translated into sounds to make a musical stir fry. The activities lead up to a celebration game in which dragon dancers try to find the Chinese leaf hidden in the recipe.

Resources

- Enlarged copy of the stir fry recipe.
- Stir fry ingredients (see recipe).
- Chopping board, knife and wok.

Preparation

Demonstrate the preparation of a stir fry using real ingredients. Invite the children to copy your actions with their hands:

> **chop** the Chinese leaf
> **slice** the mushrooms and peppers
> **stir** all the vegetables together
> **toss** (as though over a flame)

(To cook the stir fry later for the children to eat, you will need to heat the oil and soy sauce in the wok then toss the vegetables in the wok for two to three minutes over a hot flame.)

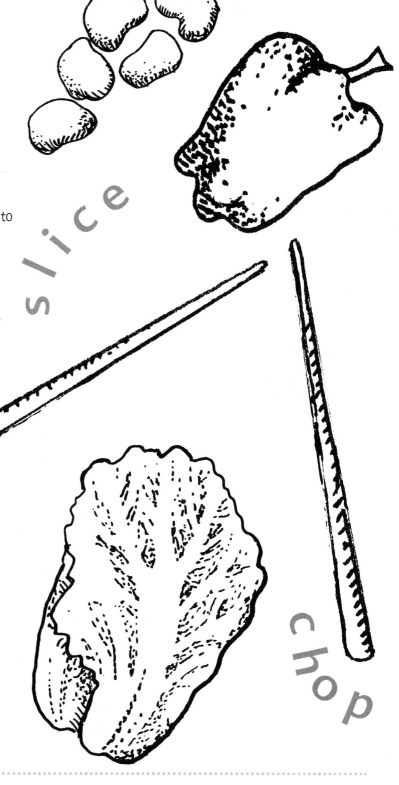

STIR FRY

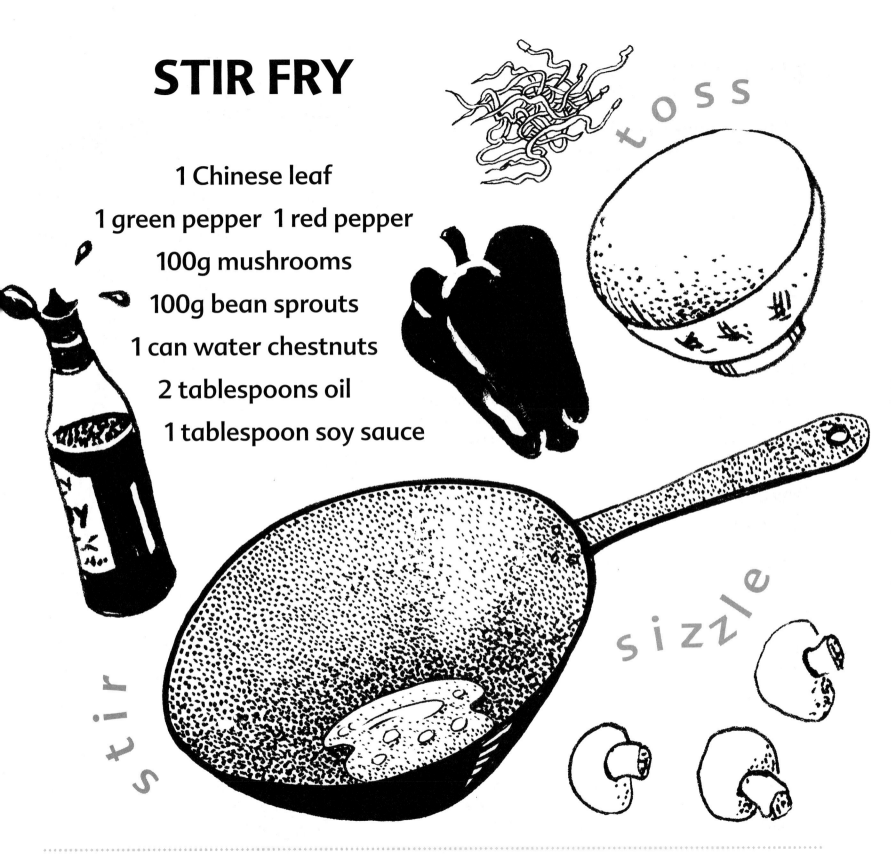

1 Chinese leaf

1 green pepper 1 red pepper

100g mushrooms

100g bean sprouts

1 can water chestnuts

2 tablespoons oil

1 tablespoon soy sauce

toss

sizzle

stir

DANCE EXPLORATION

Chinese kitchen

11 CELEBRATIONS AFTER GOOD HARVEST

Encourage the children, as they listen to the music, to repeat the four actions they have already explored – chop, slice, stir, toss.

● Develop the hand actions into larger, whole body actions, eg

chop – quick stamping patterns, co-ordinating hands and feet; sharp, strong, direct movements;

slice – use the outside edge of the hand to make straight lines;

stir – large circular movements using the body to bend, stretch and rotate;

toss – fast, explosive jumps into the air.

11 CELEBRATIONS AFTER GOOD HARVEST

Perform the whole body, cooking movements as the music plays. The children respond freely to the music, catching its bustling happy mood.

MUSIC EXPLORATION

Chinese kitchen

● Remind the children of the action words: chop, slice, stir, toss. Choose percussion sounds for each word, eg

chop – tap claves together;

slice – play a metal scraper with quick strokes of the beater; slide one cymbal or indian bell quickly across another;

stir – slowly swirl a maraca or ocean drum;

toss – slide a beater quickly across the bars of a glockenspiel from low notes to high (long bars to short); make rising 'woops' with voices and finish with a loud clap.

11 CELEBRATIONS AFTER GOOD HARVEST

The children play their action sounds along with the recording. They may play freely and in any order.

DANCE AND MUSIC DEVELOPMENT

● Each child finds a way to put the whole body actions they have explored into a simple repeatable pattern which recreates the sequence of the recipe:

chop – slice – stir – toss

● Divide into groups of four. Each group has the four instruments chosen to play the four recipe sounds.

● Allow each group time to practise the sequence.

chop   –   slice   –   stir   –   toss

● Each group takes a turn to play the sound sequence as the rest of the children perform their individual dance sequence. The dancers must listen carefully to the musicians so that they know when to change to the next action.

THE HUNGRY DRAGON GAME

The basis of this game, and the music and dance performance which follows, is the Chinese New Year tradition in which dragon dancers weave through the streets and try to catch the cabbages or Chinese leaves which are hung from upstairs windows.

Watch the video together, noticing the way the dragon moves, and responds to the music.

1. Give small groups of children turns at being part of a dragon dance. You need a 2 x 1 metre length of colourful cloth. The children stand one behind the other holding the edges of the cloth which is draped over their heads. They follow the leader who weaves around the floor space.

Try different travelling steps which can make the line move higher and lower, eg bending knees then stretching arms and body up to make the dragon's back undulate.

11 CELEBRATIONS AFTER GOOD HARVEST

The children sit in groups of four, ready to take their turn to be the dragon. Choose one group to begin. The dragon starts to move as soon as the music starts. Pause the music. The group nearest the dragon's head, dances next.

THE HUNGRY DRAGON PERFORMANCE

1. All the children sit in groups of four. Each group has a set of four stir fry instruments, one per child. One group is chosen to be the dragon first.

2. You conduct with the stir fry hand actions – in any order. The children in each group respond with the appropriate sound.

3. While the stir fry groups are playing, the dragon weaves around amongst the players. As soon as the recipe finishes, the dragon finds the nearest Chinese leaf chopper. That child leads the next group of dragon dancers. Between each turn, the groups swap their instruments around.

CROSS-CURRICULAR LINKS

Language - explore words, word patterns and poems about food.

Maths - investigate measure in recipes.
Create and remember patterns.

Science - explore change in cooking.
Learn about seasons and harvest.

Art - draw or paint Chinese rice bowls, chopsticks, teapots and food.
Make a Chinese Dragon mask.

Role play – turn the role play area into a Chinese restaurant.

PSE – invite a Chinese member of the community into school to demonstrate Chinese calligraphy.

AWAKENING

Raga Abhogi *is from India, and opens with a flute playing gentle free-flowing, exploratory music over a drone played by a tambura (stringed instrument). The tabla (pair of drums) join in and the music becomes rhythmical and energetic.*

Dance

The children tell a story in movement to describe a scene of animals sleeping, waking then dancing. The movements match the two sections of music – slow, peaceful, smooth movement, then fast rhythmical travelling.

Music

The children create music of their own with vocal sounds and instruments to tell the story. They contrast playing freely and non-rhythmically with playing a regular beat.

Resources

– A selection of small hand-held percussion instruments.

Preparation

 With the children, watch the videoclips of animal hasthas. The hastha is a traditional Indian hand gesture used in dance. Teach the seven animal hasthas, and make up memory games using the illustrations opposite to reinforce them.

 Videoclip 22 shows you one way of developing the dance idea for Awakening.

🎥 **15** tortoise
kurma hastha

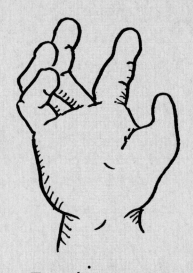

🎥 **19** tiger
viyakraha hastha

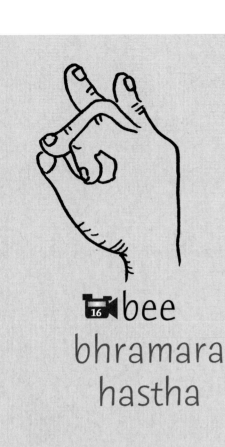

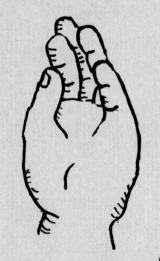 bee
bhramara
hastha

 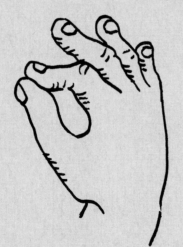 deer
simhamukha
hastha

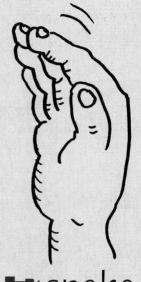 snake
sarpasirsa
hastha

elephant
mukula
hastha

hamsasya
hastha

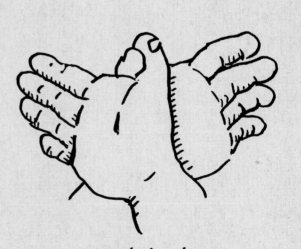 bird
garuda hastha

35

DANCE EXPLORATION

Awakening

The children start by finding sleeping shapes. Each finds a body shape which represents sleeping. Try making the shapes at different levels: low; medium; high. Rather than simply lying on the floor, try making a sleeping shape while standing, or crouching.

> **(12) RAGA ABHOGI (FIRST SECTION)**
>
> As this first section of the music plays, begin to find ways to move small parts of the body whilst remaining in shape, eg
> > fingers wiggle
> > heads roll
> > feet stretch
>
> Extend these small movements into body parts stretching away from the shape as if waking up, eg legs stretch towards the ceiling.
>
> Move smoothly and slowly into further stretches using different parts of the body, maintaining the same personal space.

The animals are awake

The sleepy, stretching shapes from Awakening now become recognisable as animals.

Select an animal hastha (either one hastha for everyone, or each child choosing their own). Each child finds ways to make the hand gestures move: in and around the children's own space; travelling in and out of each other. Lead with the hastha.

> **(13) RAGA ABHOGI (SECOND SECTION)**
>
> The animals are awake
> As the music becomes vigorous and energetic, perform the movements you have just explored.

MUSIC EXPLORATION

Awakening

- Ask the children to suggest quiet vocal sounds to accompany the smooth slow waking-up movements they have explored, eg

  mmmmmmmmmmm

  shhhhhhhhhhhhhhhh

  ahhhhhhhhhhhhhhhhh

- The children each perform these vocal sounds at the same time as they perform their Awakening movements.

The animals are awake

- Ask the children to suggest vocal sounds to represent each of the the animals, eg

  bee   **bzzzzzzzzzzzzzzzz**

  snake   **ssssssssssssssss**

  Now ask for silence. You make one of the hasthas to indicate to the children to start making the matching animal sound as quietly as possible. Repeat with a different animal.

- Divide into groups – one for each animal. Choose a child to conduct the groups with hasthas, in any order. Each group takes it in turn to make its sound and perform its corresponding movements from the 'Animals are awake' section following the order of the hand gestures.

- Repeat. This time the children each choose their own hastha and perform the movements while making the matching animal sound.

Awakening – The animals are awake

- Finally, each individual child performs the movements and sounds from both sections, moving seamlessly from one into the other.

DANCE DEVELOPMENT

The second section contains layers of beats – a very slow beat, a faster middle beat and a quick light beat. The children match their footsteps to these beats, matching also the appropriate animal.

13 RAGA ABHOGI (SECOND SECTION)

The animals are awake
As they listen, the children perform slow heavy steps to represent the elephant (they do not perform a hastha at this stage). Repeat, choosing a different animal to represent with faster lighter footwork. Repeat again with the fastest beat.

MUSIC DEVELOPMENT

● The children choose instruments to represent each of the animal movements explored above in dance, eg

| elephant | slow heavy steps |

| deer | light medium steps |

| bird | fast flying movements |

● Divide the children into small groups each representing one of the animals. The groups take turns to play. One child from each makes the animal movements while the others accompany with the appropriate beat – slow, medium, fast.

DANCE AND MUSIC PERFORMANCE

● Use tracks 12-13, or the music created by the children. (If the children use their own music, they will need to find ways to play their instruments to make Awakening music.)

Perform the two contrasting dance sections with the two sections of music – employing all the movements which have been explored and developed.

The children might wear ankle bells whilst dancing.

CROSS-CURRICULAR LINKS

Language – make a picture of the animals and their sound words. Create your own animal hasthas and tell your own story.

Maths – order the seven animals in different ways, eg largest to smallest, fastest to slowest, in groups according to number of feet. Mathematical language – smaller than, longer than, heavier than …

Art – draw or paint the chosen animals.
Make clay or plasticine models.
Make animal masks.

PSE – Read creation stories from other cultures.

DANCE FROM A DISTANT PLANET

In **Jig**, by Judith Weir, the composer imagined what would happen to a traditional tune from our planet if it were taught to aliens 'from a distant planet'. In our activity we imagined what would happen to a traditional children's dance if it were taken to a distant planet.

Dance and music

In movement and sound, the children tell the story of how a group of travelling space children make a new game out of a very old Earth one.

Resources

- A wiggly jar – a transparent jar containing beads.
- Enlarged photocopies of the body part cards – see page 40.
- A selection of small untuned percussion instruments.
- A xylophone and two beaters.

Preparation

Teach the children the Hokey Cokey (or another singing game with actions, which you know well). Sing the words and do the actions until both are firmly established, then

- perform just the actions without the words, but singing the melody to 'la';
- perform the actions in silence.

Tell the children the story opposite, showing them the pictures.

Ten little Earth children waited for their parents' starship to take them on a journey to the distant planet of Zudie-o. 'Let's play the Hokey Cokey,' said one, and they all joined in.

Months later, as the starship zoomed through space on its long journey to Zudie-o, the children said, 'Let's play the Hokey Cokey again.' But they couldn't remember the words, so they just sang the tune and did the actions.

3

Years passed and the children grew up happily on Zudie-o. They taught the Hokey Cokey to their grandchildren, and their grandchildren taught it to their grandchildren too. But they forgot the tune, and the actions got a bit jumbled up.

4

While they played, some Zudie-o children made up a new tune for the Hokey Cokey. The others liked their tune and made up some new actions.

5

An important message from Earth arrived for the Zudie-o children. 'Please come and visit us, love from Bluebell Nursery.' The children were very excited and they played their new Hokey Cokey as they waited for their starship to leave.

6

The children of Bluebell Nursery loved the new game they learned from their Zudie-o friends. They soon learnt the words and the tune, and they loved the actions.

DANCE EXPLORATION

Wiggly jar

You need the wiggly jar and the body part cards.

- Show the children the wiggly jar and explain that when they see and hear the beads moving, they wiggle their fingers. When the jar is still, everyone freezes.

- Move a different part of the body to the sound of the wiggly jar.

- Place the body cards face down. Point to the children in turn to pick up a card and demonstrate an action with that part of the body for the others to follow when the wiggly jar moves, freezing each time it stops. Change to a new card.

---

14 JIG

You need the body cards again.

You hold all the cards. Show the first to the children and explain that as soon as they hear the music they move that part of the body. Freeze each time there is a silence.

Change to another card when you choose. (Gauge this by watching the children's response. With practice you may be able to change the cards more frequently.)

Repeat without the cards – the children make up their own minds which part of the body to move each time they hear music.

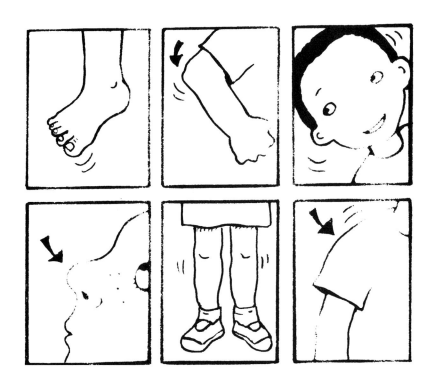

MUSIC EXPLORATION

Wiggly jar

Distribute a small untuned percussion instrument to each child.

- Play the wiggly jar game with instruments. When they see/hear the jar, the children respond with light, fast, short sounds on their instruments. As soon as the jar stops, the instruments stop and must be kept silent until the jar moves again.

- Play the game with a xylophone taking the place of the wiggly jar. One child comes out and improvises using two beaters on the xylophone. The children respond by joining in with their untuned percussion.

The soloist explores different ways of playing:

- sliding the beater across the bars
- rapidly tapping any bars
- tapping on one note
- playing pairs of notes

The others find ways to respond using their untuned instruments. As soon as the xylophone player stops, the others stop and must be silent.

DANCE AND MUSIC DEVELOPMENT

You need a xylophone and two beaters.

- In a circle, find a sequence of five movements which everyone can remember, eg

  1. shake hands vigorously above the head - FREEZE
  2. stretch hands out to the side wiggling hips - FREEZE
  3. crouch down low and nod head - FREEZE
  4. rise in short jerks - FREEZE
  5. wobble into the circle and out again

- Now find sounds to match the movements. Invite a child to play the xylophone. While the others perform the action, the child finds sounds which match the movement, eg

  1. quickly tap any high-pitched bars with alternate beaters. Stop immediately the action stops.

  During the silent, motionless pause, the child quietly joins the others, passing the beaters to the next child you indicate, who makes up new sounds to match the next movement, and so on.

- When you have found a satisfactory sequence of sounds to match the movements of the dance, perform the new dance, accompanying it with the new tune, played by one child or by five, taking turns to play.

PERFORMANCE

You tell the story while a group of ten children perform the actions to it. Use the story and pictures from pages 38-39. In the last part of the story, everyone joins in dancing the new Hokey Cokey.

CROSS-CURRICULAR LINKS

Language – write a letter to Bluebell Nursery thanking them for the visit. Write down the instructions for the Hokey Cokey, or for the new dance, so that no one forgets it next time.
Look at ways of changing words, eg pan to cot (pan – pat – pot – cot).
Pass a whispered message round the circle – is it the same at the end?

Maths – use positional language (in, out, up, down).
Investigate large numbers, eg the distance of the planets from earth.

Science – investigate space travel and the planets. Visit the NASA website (www.nasa.gov).

ICT – use the robot toy, Roamer, to move forwards and backwards, and turn right and left.

DT and art – design and make a planet landscape for use with play people and construction kit rockets. Make a night-sky background, using black paper and chalk or pastels.

A group of children dance and sing the Hokey Cokey.

The children dance the Hokey Cokey without the words, singing to 'la'.

The children perform the actions in a jumbled-up way – in silence.

The children make up new actions and accompany them with new xylophone music.

The children are invited to visit Bluebell Nursery. They practise their new Hokey Cokey.

Everyone copies the new game.

PARACHUTE

Bransle de chevaux *is an old French dance, first written down at the end of the 16th century. On this recording the music is played by bagpipes, hurdy gurdy, recorder and other early wind instruments. The Bransle was the most popular dance of its time, performed both indoors and out, in court or at country festivals.*

Dance

The children learn to perform a simple circle dance, with or without a parachute. They adapt their movements to match the changing speed of the music.

Music

The children play a steady beat at different speeds using untuned and tuned instruments.

Resources

- A parachute if you have one.
- One group of wood instruments, eg woodblock, claves, castanets.
- One group of skin instruments, eg tambours and drums with soft beaters.
- Chime bars G and D.

Preparation

With or without a parachute, play simple circle games such as Ring a Roses or The Mulberry Bush to give the children practice in –

> forming a circle holding hands;
> moving together clockwise and anti-clockwise;
> changing direction and stopping together;
> working co-operatively.

 Familiarise yourself with the Parachute dance.

COUNT	1	2	3	4	5	6	7	8	1	2	3	4	5	6	7	8	
first section: skin and drone																	
STEP LEFT	L	L	L	L	L	L	L	L	L	L	L	L	L	L	L	L	STOP!
STEP RIGHT	R	R	R	R	R	R	R	R	R	R	R	R	R	R	R	R	STOP!
second section: skin and drone								HEY!								HEY!	
STEP IN STEP OUT	I	I	I	I	I	I	I	I	O	O	O	O	O	O	O		
	I	I	I	I	I	I	I	I	O	O	O	O	O	O	O	HEY!	HEY!
third section: wood and drone																	
SHAKE PARA-CHUTE GENTLY	U	D	U	D	U	D	U	D	U	D	U	D	U	D	U		STOP!
BOUNCE	V	V	V	V	V	V	V	V	V	V	V	V	V	V	V		STOP!

PERFORM TO CD TRACK 15 (The dance is repeated three times, stopping the third time after the second section)

DANCE EXPLORATION

You need a tambour and soft beater, and a parachute if you have one.

● Tap a steady beat on the wooden **rim** of a tambour with the stick of the beater and ask the children to step on the spot in time to it. Try speeding up a little or slowing down, noticing how the children match their steps to the beat. As they become more confident and able, play the beat faster – up to jogging speed.

● Now tap the **skin** of the tambour with the soft head of the beater and ask the children to travel around the space. Again gradually change the speed until they can all walk and jog to the beat.

● Alternate the stepping-on-the-spot signal (tambour **rim**) with the travelling signal (tambour **skin**). Check that all the children are able to respond to the change.

● Form a circle holding hands or holding a parachute. (You will need a helper in the circle.) Let the children with their helper practise ways of travelling together in a circle whilst maintaining the hand hold and while you beat the tambour skin. Tell the children how the circle will move, eg 'Step to the left' , 'Step to the middle', 'Step out again'. Between each change tap the tambour rim to signal the children to step on the spot.

MUSIC EXPLORATION

Metal, wood, skin game

1. Divide into three groups in a circle, with these instruments (you will also need your tambour and beater):

Group 1 – pairs of chime bars G + D (plus pairs of beaters)

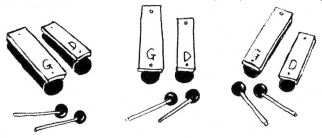

Group 2 – wood: woodblocks and sticks, claves or finger castanets

Group 3 – skin: tambours or small drums tapped with fingertips

2. Start the chime bar group first by clapping a steady beat. The children pick up the beat, playing

    G D G D G D G D
(or the other way round – D G D G, or playing both notes together).

This is called a drone and is what the bagpipe plays throughout the Bransle without changing – literally 'droning on'.

3. The chime bars continue. Signal the wood group to take up the beat by calling 'Wood', and playing the **rim** of your own tambour, while stepping on the spot.

4. When you call 'Skin', the wood group stops playing and the skin group starts. Reinforce this by tapping the **skin** of your tambour and stepping around the circle.

5. Play the game at different speeds.

6. A confident child may conduct by stepping on the spot or stepping around the circle.

DANCE AND MUSIC DEVELOPMENT

15 BRANSLE DE CHEVAUX

Teach the dance using the chart and the recorded music, and using a parachute if you have one.

Three children - metal, wood and skin - play along with the music. One child plays the chime bar pattern throughout, keeping in time to the music. The wood and skin children respond to the dancers movements, playing or not playing according to whether the dancers are travelling or stepping on the spot.

MAKE UP YOUR OWN DANCE

- Make up your own circle dance with or without a parachute by

  - changing the order of the actions;
  - substituting new actions.

- Change the formation from a circle to a line (no parachute) as a whole class or in small groups. Move side by side holding hands or stepping one behind the other. The line can move from side to side, forward or back, by spiralling in and out, or in curving/snaking floor patterns.

CROSS-CURRICULAR LINKS

Language - write down the instructions for the new game or dance. Write a stick poem called Parachute or Sky Diver.

Maths - sequencing with 1-8: count forwards and back; what comes next; one less than one more than; recognise the numerals 1-8. Talk about the clock face - what is clockwise/anticlockwise? Divide a circle into half, quarter, etc, and colour with a repeating pattern. With older children, use 90 or 45 degree angles to divide the circle.

Art - look at pictures of parachutes; design a logo with a parachute theme for your school - paint it using the colour spectrum.

PSE - talk about teamwork and co-operation whilst playing with the parachute; play parachute games that encourage co-operation.

Science - investigate how the parachute behaves in different ways during the dance.

CIRCUS RING

Circus music by Aaron Copland is a dramatic and colourful musical picture of circus performers.

There are three sections. The first and last are grand and expansive, evoking acts such as the trapeze, the tightrope and acrobatics. The middle section is a madcap whirl of laughing clowns and skilful jugglers. Each section ends with the whole orchestra playing 'Da daa' like a ringmaster's triumphant pose at the end of an act.

Dance and music

Through exploration, the children find movements and sounds to represent human circus acts. For example they contrast the slow, strong, graceful swing of the trapeze artists with the fast and lively hand movements of jugglers. These and other movements and sounds may be developed into a performance with three contrasting sections punctuated by the ring master's 'Da daa'.

Resources

– A range of tuned and untuned percussion instruments.

Preparation

Some children may never have seen a circus. Show them a video (eg Cirque du Soleil) or pictures, or use poetry and stories to familiarise them with trapeze and tightrope acts, acrobats, jugglers and clowns. Check that they are aware of the ringmaster's role.

fast

skilful

graceful

fun

proud

DANCE EXPLORATION

Explore movements for each section; first without the music then with it. Use the children's own ideas for acts as well as those given here.

Grand opening

- Use whole body movements to explore the range of actions in trapeze, tightrope-walking, acrobatics, eg

trapeze	swinging forwards, backwards, side to side
tightrope	travelling carefully along thin lines; turning on the spot;
acrobats	balancing on different parts of the body; jumping along; jumping high to make shapes in the air.

- All find strong, bold ringmaster poses which are still. Whenever you say a loud 'Da daa' and strike your bold pose, everyone moves into a still bold pose of their own.

- Repeat this but choose a different child each time to be the ringmaster. Challenge the children to hold their 'Da daa' pose as still as they can.

16 CIRCUS MUSIC (FIRST SECTION)

While the music plays, all perform the movements you have explored . Strike your bold, still poses when the orchestra plays 'Da Daa' at the end.

- Repeat the music a number of times. Encourage the children to explore the movements further by choosing some favourite actions and linking them together into phrases, which can be remembered and repeated, eg

swing forward and back – travel forward – spin on the spot

Jugglers and clowns

- Now try out the quick actions of jugglers and clowns, eg

throwing and catching balls;
wobbling and falling.

Perform these smaller movements quickly and repeatedly.

- Appoint a ringmaster to signal 'Da Daa' as before.

17 CIRCUS MUSIC (SECOND SECTION)

Perform the movements you have explored. Strike your bold, still poses when the orchestra plays 'Da Daa'. Repeat a number of times.

16-18 CIRCUS MUSIC (COMPLETE)

Perform all three sections from the beginning, including the Grand Finale section which repeats the opening.

MUSIC EXPLORATION

Discover different ways of playing percussion instruments in response to the dance movements you have found.

Circus ring game

1. The children sit in a large circle, each with a percussion instrument placed in front of them on the floor.

2. Select an act and choose one child to come into the ring and perform one movement from it. Try out some different sounds to accompany the movement, eg

run a beater over the bars of a glockenspiel or xylophone in big sweeps from top to bottom to top

shake a maraca continuously

tap a two-tone woodblock quickly on alternate sides

3. Appoint a ringmaster and all practise playing 'Da Daa' on the instruments when the ringmaster strikes a bold pose.

4. Choose some children to take turns to perform their linked movement phrases. The other children respond in sound, changing when the movement changes. All play 'Da Daa' or strike a bold pose as the ringmaster signals the end of an act.

DANCE DEVELOPMENT AND PERFORMANCE

Working in pairs, the children develop the whole body actions for Grand opening/finale and the smaller, quicker movements of Jugglers and clowns. First make pairs, standing together or apart in any of these formations:

side by side

facing each other

back to back

 Each pair chooses a set of movements for the opening and finale, and a contrasting set of quick light movements for the middle section. They work together on performing them one after the other, closing each with 'Da Daa'.

16-18 CIRCUS MUSIC (COMPLETE)

In pairs, perform the chosen movements to the music.

MUSIC AND DANCE PERFORMANCE

The children make pieces of circus music to accompany a pair of dancers.

● Choose one pair of dancers. Divide everyone else into three groups of musicians.

● The groups take it in turns to work with the dance pair. They respond in sound to their movements to create three sections of music – Grand opening, Jugglers and clowns, Grand Finale. The groups each appoint a ringmaster to signal 'Da Daa' for the end of each section.

CROSS-CURRICULAR LINKS

Language – use alliteration to think of names for circus performers, eg Carol Clown, Jimmy Juggler; make a list of rhyming words (including nonsense words), eg clown, frown, down; write some jokes to make each other laugh.

Maths – make a 'tightrope' by supporting each end of a strip of card on a play brick. How many play people can fit on the rope before it collapses; will different strengths of card make any difference? Time or count how long you can balance on one leg/walk balancing a large ball on your hand/bounce a ball.

PSE – talk about the skills the circus performers have developed, and how hard they have persevered to perfect them.

Art – make a clown mask or design his or her costume; design a poster to announce the arrival of the circus.

Role play – use appropriate clown props to make up your own circus performances; make swings, tightropes and other props to go in a group-made circus ring.

JACK AND THE GIANT

Contredanse is a lively piece of orchestral dance music from 18th century France. The first section of the music (A) is repeated several times. In between, there are contrasting sections, making this pattern:

A B A C A D A E A F A

The story of Jack and the beanstalk falls well into this pattern. The repeated A section always represents the giant, while the Jack episodes of the story take place in the contrasting sections between.

Dance and music

The children tell the story first in a song and a fingerplay, then in whole body movements to the recorded music, and finally they recreate the story in a musical performance game.

Resources

- Enlarged copies of the story cards opposite. Write the letter name on the back of each for quick reference.
- A selection of small percussion instruments such as rattles, maracas, tambours, hand drums, wood blocks.

Preparation

Remind the children of the story then tell it in the simplified outline given in the story cards opposite:

A Once there was a giant who lived above the clouds.
B A little beanstalk began to grow up into the sky.
C Jack climbed the beanstalk.
D Jack was amazed as he looked all about him.
E He wanted to explore the castle he saw in the distance. He was scared. He crept up on tiptoe.
F Out jumped the giant. Jack ran back down the beanstalk, hiding behind the leaves as he escaped.

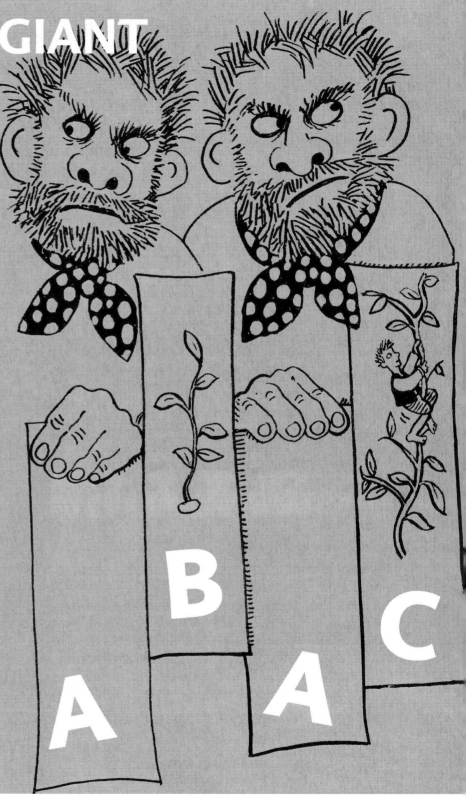

(preparation continued)

Preparation continued

27

19 THE GIANT'S SONG

Listen to the giant's song, tapping alternate knees with fists to the beat of the music (words in bold). Some children will be able to join in with the song though they don't need to at this stage.

Fiddledee **fid**dledee **fid**dledee **fum**
I am the **gi**ant and **I'm** so **hun**gry!
Fiddledee **fid**dledee **fid**dledee **fum**
Live humans to **fill** my **tum**!

Jack's episodes in fingerplay

 B - weave hand upwards

 C - climb fingers up arm

 D - shade eyes with hand

  E - tiptoe fingers along horizontal forearm

F - climb fingers down arm, curl up and hide

Put the story together. You (and any children who want to) sing the giant's song. Everyone taps knees. At the end of the song, hold up the first Jack card, while the children make the fingerplay actions. Sing again then hold up the next card. Repeat this until the children know the sequence well and can play it without the cards.

20 CONTREDANSE

You will hear the giant's song played by the orchestra. While the A section plays, tap knees firmly as in the song. Next you hear the B section - the bean growing. Make the fingerplay actions you have devised. Tap knees for the next A section, then fingerplay section C, and so on through to the end.

DANCE EXPLORATION

28

Explore whole body movements to replace the fingerplay actions:

A — THE GIANT

Find different giant movements. Experiment with:

travelling movements	stamping, striding, jumping;
strong body shapes	large, angular, wide, balanced;
arm and hand gestures	fists, pushing, swinging.

B — THE BEAN GROWS

Move from low to high using different parts of the body (fingertips, elbow, nose) to lead upwards. Move slowly and carefully.

C — CLIMBING THE BEANSTALK

Use stretching movements which reach and pull, finding ways to do them at a high level.

D — EXPLORING ABOVE THE CLOUDS

Move around the whole space, responding to the words

over	jump, stretch, step;
under	roll, crawl, slide;
through	wiggle, squeeze;

E — APPROACHING THE CASTLE

Tiptoe quietly in and around each other, always looking, turning the head from side to side, and changing direction.

F — ESCAPING DOWN THE BEANSTALK

Make quick descending movements, showing changes of speed and stopping in shapes which convey the idea of hiding, eg small, curled shapes.

20 CONTREDANSE (SECTION A)

Make the giant's movements in time to the strong beat of the music during the A section.

20 CONTREDANSE (SECTIONS B-F)

One by one, scroll to the beginning of each section of Jack's music. Explore Jack's movements as above, responding to the sounds in the music.

MUSIC EXPLORATION

Give each child a small percussion instrument. With these, they find sounds to describe the story:

A — THE GIANT

19 THE GIANT'S SONG

Replace the fist tapping with playing instruments on the beat. The children may step on the spot or move around in time to the strong beat of the music as they play.

Jack's episodes

Choose one or more children to repeat the movements they have explored in dance, while the other children respond to the movements in sound. Here are some suggestions.

B — THE BEAN GROWS

Seated again, the children use their instruments to find quiet leafy, rustling sounds. As the bean grows the sounds get louder.

C — CLIMBING THE BEANSTALK

With instruments placed on the floor in front of them, the children use just their voices to find rising, climbing sounds, responding to Jack's movements.

D — EXPLORING ABOVE THE CLOUDS

Find different ways to play the instruments; be inquisitive and explorative with them to create a sound picture of an unusual, unfamiliar new world for Jack to explore.

E — APPROACHING THE CASTLE

Find the quietest way of playing the instruments, eg fingertip tapped gently on tambourine skin or jingle.

F — ESCAPING DOWN THE BEANSTALK

Use voices and instruments freely, playing lightly and quickly in response to Jack climbing quickly down the beanstalk, and stopping in silence at times to hide.

JACK AND THE GIANT PERFORMANCE GAME

In this game, music and dance are combined to tell the story.

1. Each child has an instrument as before, and all sit in a wide circle. Place Jack's story cards face down in order in the centre of the ring.

2. Choose a child to move like the giant. Start the game by all singing or tapping the Giant's song. During the song, the giant stomps around the outside of the circle. On 'TUM', he or she stops and points to the closest child in the ring. The giant sits down.

3. The chosen child goes into the centre and turns up the first of Jack's cards. This child then dances the episode of the story while the others play (or use their voices).

4. Pick another giant from the ring, and repeat until all the cards have been turned up.

5. Finish with the song, but change the last line to –

No humans to **fill** my **tum**!

The last giant mimes his hunger.

CROSS-CURRICULAR LINKS

Language. Explore other versions of the story; describe the giant's appearance and character.
Extend vocabulary by collecting as many words as possible for 'big' and 'small'.

PSE - describe Jack's feelings.

Science - grow a bean, observing and measuring the different stages of growth.

Maths - record the structure of the music in graphic symbols. Compare and sort sizes and use appropriate mathematical vocabulary to describe reasons for sorting.

Art - make a colourful frieze of the story.

DANCE GLOSSARY

basic actions – the words used to describe what the body is doing, eg locomotion, turning, jumping, stillness, gesture (see separate definitions below).

context – the particular situation and circumstance which will help the meaning and intention of the dance.

contrast – movements, shapes, dynamics which are clearly quite different to each other, eg fast v slow, light v heavy, high v low.

curling – a movement initiated by shortening the muscles and drawing towards and around the centre of the body.

direction – moving to the front, back, or to the side.

dynamics – a variety of combined qualities used to colour a movement, eg explosive jump, peaceful travelling.

expression – to perform movements with dynamics and with an understanding of the idea to be communicated.

gesture – in which a particular part or parts of the body does an action without transferring any weight, eg nod of the head, shrug of the shoulders.

interpret – show understanding in a specified way.

jumping – movement in which the whole body is elevated off the ground.

level – the height at which a movement is performed, eg floor, low, middle, high.

locomotion – movement in which the whole body travels.

motif – a simple phrase or shape that contains something which can be repeated, varied and developed.

phrase – a 'sentence' of movement which has a clear shape in time and an ending.

quality – a movement's quality is determined by its use of time (fast/slow), weight (light/heavy), flow (bound/free), space (direct/flexible).

represent – to interpret through movement an animal, idea or character as opposed to miming the action or 'pretending to be'.

sequence – one movement followed by another leading to patterns of movement.

shape – achieved when the body holds and maintains a position in space.

stillness – in which the whole body pauses motionless.

stimulus – a starting point for the initiation and exploration of movement.

stretching – in which the range of a movement is increased by lengthening the muscles away from the centre of the body.

tableau – a picture created by bodies holding shapes in space.

tradition – something which has existed before, and has been handed on.

turning – movement in which the whole body rotates.

The artistic process

develop – altering the action, space, time, or quality of movements to build longer phrases, extend motifs and construct sections or whole dances.

explore – exploring movement imaginatively in response to guided tasks.

formation – the organisation of bodies (dancers) in space to create different designs, eg circle/line, eg Parachute.

improvise – immediate or unplanned response to a stimulus or task.

refine – to practise and remember movement in order to improve it.

structure – the form of a whole dance which organises the movement, phrases or motifs into a complete dance, eg narrative storytelling as in Jack and the Giant.

type – a broad classification of dances:
> **abstract dance**, eg *Circles* (based in movement itself)
> **comic dance**, eg *Dance from a Distant Planet* (depicting humour)
> **dance drama/narrative dance**, eg *Jack and the Giant* a storytelling dance)
> **dramatic dance**, eg *Circus Ring* (use of character and relationships)
> **traditional dance**, eg *Awakening* (roots of dance in culture and tradition)

ACKNOWLEDGEMENTS

The following copyright holders have kindly given their permission for the inclusion of their copyright material in this book and CD pack.

Every effort has been made to trace and acknowledge copyright owners. If any right has been omitted, the publishers offer their apologies and will rectify this in subsequent editions following notification.

All rights of the producer and of the owner of the works reproduced reserved. Unauthorised copying, hiring, lending, public performance and broadcasting of these recordings and videoclips prohibited.

AUDIO TRACKS

Zudie-o (melody traditional, words arranged by Helen MacGregor for this edition) performed by Vivien Ellis and Missak Takoushian, recorded by David Moses. Ⓟ 2001 A & C Black.

Recording of piece from the Watermusic by Handel - **Country Dance** from Suite no 3 in G. Performed by the Bath Festival Orchestra, conducted by Yehudi Menuhin. Recording © 1964. Classics for Pleasure cat no CD CFP 4698. Digital remastering Ⓟ 1989 by EMI Records Ltd.

Mare Tranquillitatis composed and performed by Vangelis. Courtesy of BMG Entertainment International UK and Ireland Limited.

The Snow is Dancing (from Children's Corner Suite by Claud Debussy) and **Playful Pizzicato** (from Simple Symphony by Benjamin Britten). Courtesy of Deutche Gramaphon. Licensed by kind permission from The Film & TV Licensing Division, part of the Universal Music Group.

Kantele (Konevistan Kirkonkellet – Bells of Konevista Monastery), running time 2.58, artists - Martti Pokela, Eeva-Leena, Pokela, Matti Konito; composer: traditional from Karelia Finland, arrangers, Martti Pokela, Eeva-Leena, Pokela, Matti Konito, publishers M/s. Ⓟ 1978 Finlandia Records/Warner Music Finland, original recording SFLP 8578/A8, available on 3984-21835-2.

Celebrations after good harvest (Qing Feng Shou) performed by Bainigan Village Orchestra from World Music. This recording has been taken from the Auvidis Unesco World Music © Auvidis/Unesco, Ⓟ Auvidis/Unesco.

Raga abhogi performed by Haiprasad Chaurasia from World Music (BBC Music Magazine) taken from The Raga Guide on the Nimbus Records Label. Ⓟ Nimbus Records Limited.

Jig (from Airs from another planet) 2. 14, by Judith Weir © Novello & Co Ltd Ⓟ 1986. Sound recording © Lontano Records Ltd 1992.

Bransle de Chevaux courtesy of Archiv. Licensed by kind permission from the Film & TV Licensing Division, part of the Universal Music Group.

Circus Music by Aaron Copeland, performed by The Saint Louis Symphony Orchestra and conducted by Leonard Slatkin. Courtesy of BMG Classics US.

Contredanse (from Les Indes Galantes by J.P. Rameau). Courtesy of Philips. Licensed by kind permission from the Film & TV Licensing Division, part of the Universal Music Group.

VIDEOCLIPS

Chinese dragon courtesy of BSkyB Ltd.

Moon walking courtesy of NASA.

All other videoclips filmed by Jamie Acton-Bond for A & C Black, © 2001 A & C Black:

Zudie-o performed by the staff and children of Kintore Way Nursery School.

Kitchen fun, **Parachute**, **Circus ring** and **Jack and the Giant** performed by the staff and children of Grafton Infant School.

Moon walking actions, **The snow is dancing**, **Circles**, **In the garden** performed by the staff and children of Northbury Infant School.

Animal hasthas for **Awakening** demonstrated and performed by Shaila Thiru and the children of the Asian Women's Association classical Indian dance class.

All other demonstrations performed by Bobbie Gargrave, Jake Body and Chellayne Coggins.

Snowman illustration by Dee Shulman animated by Adrian Downie.

SPECIAL THANKS

The authors and publishers gratefully acknowledge the many people who have assisted in the development of **Let's go Zudie-o**. In particular they wish to thank: Elsa Acton-Bond, Sue Baskill and the staff and children of Grafton Infant School, Jake Body and Chellayne Coggins of Dagenham Priory School, Adrian Downie, Vivien Ellis, Sue Johnston, Jenny Liggins and the staff and children of Kintore Way Nursery School, Roger Mitchell and the staff and children of Northbury Infant School, David Moses, Ann Nash, Ann Peet, Michelle Simpson, Missak Takoushian, Shaila Thiru and the Asian Women's Centre and children of the classical Indian dance class, Nikki Tilson, Tina Tong, Zoe Wigglesworth.

Thanks are also due to the London Boroughs of Barking and Dagenham, and Southwark.

INDEX OF VIDEOCLIPS

Let's go zudie-o

Clip_01
Children perform the Zudie-o dance.

Upbeat

Clip_02
Demonstrating the use of play equipment.

Moon walking

Clip_03
Astronauts walk on the moon. Apollo moon landing footage.

Clip_04
Children demonstrate fast and slow hand actions.

Clip_05
Children demonstrate whole body moon walking actions which travel.

The snow is dancing

Clip_06
Animation of the snowman illustration on pages 16-17.

Clip_07
Children demonstrate a snow dance exploration.

Circles

Clip_08
Making small circles while three notes are repeated.

Clip_09
Making larger circles while five notes are repeated.

Clip_10
Making large, travelling circles while seven notes are repeated.

In the garden

Clip_11
Children explore the movements of bees, butterflies and grasshoppers.

Clip_12
Three 'gardeners' demonstrate different types of working movement.

Kitchen fun

Clip_13
Chop, slice, stir, toss movement explorations.

Clip_14
Dragon dancers hunt for Chinese leaf in the streets of Soho.

Awakening

The animal hasthas are demonstrated individually:

Clip_15	Tortoise
Clip_16	Bee
Clip_17	Deer
Clip_18	Snake
Clip_19	Tiger
Clip_20	Elephant
Clip_21	Bird

Clip_22
Children, with their teacher, explore an 'awakening' dance.

Parachute

Clip_23
Children and their teachers perform the bransle, using a parachute.

Circus ring

Clip_24
Children perform a 'Grand opening' sequence of movements.

Clip_25
The ringmaster pose.

Clip_26
Children perform a 'Jugglers and clowns' sequence.

Jack and the giant

Clip_27
Children and their teachers sing the Giant's song.

Clip_28
Performance of a complete sequence of Jack and the Giant.